Happy Ever After

For Ellie
S.W.

Bradman, Tony

Goldilocks and
the Just Right
Club / Tony
                    JS

1619682

ORCHARD BOOKS
338 Euston Road, London NW1 3BH
Orchard Books Australia
Hachette Children's Books
Level 17/207, Kent Street, Sydney, NSW 2000

ISBN 1 84362 530 X (hardback)
ISBN 1 84362 538 5 (paperback)
First published in Great Britain in 2006
First paperback publication in 2006

Text © Tony Bradman 2006
Illustrations © Sarah Warburton 2006

1 3 5 7 9 10 8 6 4 2 (hardback)
1 3 5 7 9 10 8 6 4 2 (paperback)
Printed in Great Britain

Tony Bradman

Happy Ever After

GOLDILOCKS
AND THE JUST RIGHT CLUB

Illustrated by Sarah Warburton

ORCHARD BOOKS

Goldilocks felt sick as they came round the corner and she saw her house. Mum and Dad were going to be seriously unhappy.

After all, she *was* being marched
home by a cross grown-up. And judging
by her frown as she rapped on the front
door, Mrs Bear was still very cross.

"Goldilocks sweetheart, where have you been?" said Mum.

"Er...hi there," said Dad, noticing Mrs Bear. "And you are?"

"Mrs Bear," she said. "Your daughter broke into our cottage."

"She did WHAT?" said Dad, horrified.
"Is this true, young lady?"

Goldilocks glanced up at him, nodded and burst into tears...

Mrs Bear told Mum and Dad the whole story, and soon they were frowning too.

Mum and Dad said they were
sorry, and that they couldn't
understand it because Goldilocks
was a good girl, and that they
would pay for the damage.

And Goldilocks said she was sorry
as well.

Mrs Bear seemed satisfied with that,
although she still looked pretty stern and
grumpy when she left. Goldilocks was
glad to see her go.

"I'll bet it was some kind of silly dare," Mum said. "You were with a group of friends, someone suggested it, things got out of hand..."

"No, Mum," said Goldilocks between
sniffs. "I was on my own."

Goldilocks would have loved to be part of a group of friends at school. But she'd never found the right group, and didn't know why.

Today she'd felt so unhappy about
it she'd gone off into the woods after
school instead of coming straight home.

And the Bears' Cottage had been
very tempting...

She knew she'd been very naughty.
But climbing trees and splashing in
muddy streams had been a lot of fun.

And trying on Mrs Bear's clothes and experimenting with her make-up had been cool, too.

"You're not unhappy at school, are you?" asked Dad.

Goldilocks didn't answer. Mum and Dad looked at each other and raised their eyebrows...

...and by the end of the week, they'd arranged for her to transfer to a new school.

Goldilocks was surprised, but pleased.
It might be a chance for her to find
some friends at last...

She felt excited when she said goodbye to her parents and walked into Forest Primary. But she was nervous, too.

"OK, settle down everybody," said
Miss Sweet, her new teacher. The
children fell silent. "I'd like to introduce
you to Goldilocks, your new classmate.
I'm sure you'll do your best to make her
feel welcome."

Goldilocks smiled shyly. Thirty pairs of eyes stared back at her, but nobody spoke. Miss Sweet tutted, and made the whole class say hello.

"Don't worry, dear," she whispered to
Goldilocks. "Just be yourself, and I'm
sure you'll fit right in…"

At playtime, Goldilocks stood in the
playground watching everyone.

"Hi," a smiling girl said eventually. "I'm Little Red Riding Hood, and this is Baby Bear. We were wondering if you'd like to play with us."

"Actually, we've met before, in my bedroom," Baby Bear said eagerly. "It was all a bit confusing, so you probably don't remember me."

"We like to play pretending games, don't we?" said Little Red Riding Hood. "Today we're deadly Ninja warriors on a special mission..."

"Er...thanks," said Goldilocks. "But no thanks."

Little Red Riding Hood and Baby Bear looked disappointed and walked off.

Little Red Riding Hood seemed pretty cool, thought Goldilocks. But if she made friends with Baby Bear she might have to meet scary Mrs Bear again...

Besides, she had decided on the group for her - the Princesses. That's what she called them, anyway.

Their names were Maisy, Daisy,
Molly, Polly and Scarlett, and they
were the prettiest, most fashionable girls
in the class. They spent every playtime
brushing each other's hair and talking
about clothes. Goldilocks thought they'd
be just right...

And they were - for a while. But after a couple of days she began to feel, well...that something was wrong. She liked being girly, but now she realised she could get very bored with it, too.

Then one morning it poured with rain, and at lunchtime the playground was covered with puddles. Goldilocks couldn't resist stamping in them and getting wet and muddy, and soon she was having lots of fun.

But the Princesses were not impressed.

"Oh dear, she's obviously not our kind of person after all, girls..." said Scarlett snootily, and the five of them turned their backs on her.

Goldilocks was upset, but then she
thought that maybe it was a good
thing. So the next day she stood in the
playground watching everyone again.
Soon Little Red Riding Hood and Baby
Bear came up to her.

"Hey, would you like to do some skipping with us?" said Baby Bear.

"You must be joking," Goldilocks muttered. She still felt the same about Baby Bear, and she thought they'd stop pestering her if she wasn't nice. Besides, she had already found another group she liked the look of.

She called them the Troll Boys. Their names were Benny, Lenny, Harry, Barry and Jake, and they were the loudest, cheekiest boys in her class.

They spent every playtime running around making as much noise as they could. Goldilocks thought they would be just right...

And they were - for a while. But soon
she got the same feeling as before.
Something about this was wrong, too.

She enjoyed being one of the boys.
But now she realised she could get very
bored with it as well.

Then one playtime the Troll Boys decided they were going to have a belching contest. They thought it was hilarious...but Goldilocks didn't.

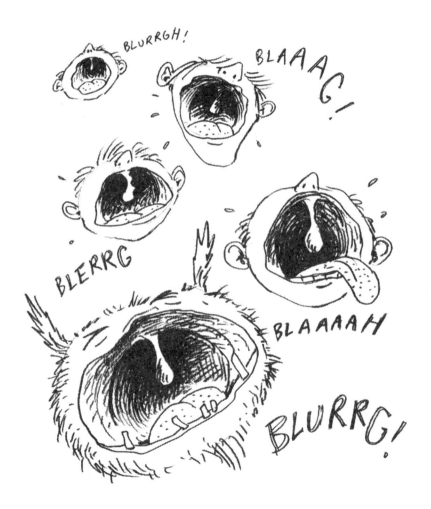

"Ugh, that's disgusting," she said. "Count me out."

"Suit yourself," Jake said rudely. "Come on lads, she probably wants to...brush her hair." And the five of them turned their backs on her.

That evening Goldilocks sat in her bedroom feeling glum. She was starting to think she would never be part of a group of friends.

"Just be yourself," Miss Sweet had said. But how could she do that? Girls didn't seem to like one side of her, and boys didn't seem to like the other.

She realised now that was why she'd never fitted in at her old school, and why her afternoon in the woods had been such fun.

She'd been adventurous in the woods
and girly in the Bears' cottage, all on
the same day. Maybe she needed some
friends who liked both sides of her...

Suddenly she thought of Little Red
Riding Hood and Baby Bear.
Little Red Riding Hood talking
about pretending to be a deadly
Ninja warrior...

...Baby Bear happy to skip with her...why, they didn't seem to mind what they played, so long as they had fun! They would be perfect.

She would just have to take the risk of meeting Mrs Bear again. So the next day, at playtime, Goldilocks went straight up to Little Red Riding Hood and Baby Bear...and asked if she could play with them.

"Although I'd understand if you didn't want anything to do with me," she said nervously. "I mean, I know I wasn't very nice to you before."

"Really?" said Little Red Riding Hood, puzzled. "I didn't notice." Then she smiled, and so did Baby Bear, and they all went off together...

Goldilocks really enjoyed playing with
her new friends. Little Red Riding Hood
liked doing girly stuff, but she had an
adventurous side as well. After all, she
did do karate.

And Baby Bear was a real boy, but
he didn't mind playing house or holding
one end of a skipping rope.

And once she got to know Goldilocks
properly, Mrs Bear turned out to be
a bit of a softie. Although she always
kept a careful eye on things...

The only problem Goldilocks had was
trying to choose a name for the three of
them. But then it came to her...

They weren't too girly or too rough - they were *The Just Right Club.* So Goldilocks (and Mum and Dad when they got her school report at the end of term) lived...

HAPPILY EVER AFTER!

Happy Ever After

Written by Tony Bradman
Illustrated by Sarah Warburton

These books are available from all good bookshops, or can be ordered direct
from the publisher: Orchard Books, PO BOX 29, Douglas IM99 1BQ.
Credit card orders please telephone 01624 836000 or fax 01624 837033 or
visit our Internet site: www.wattspub.co.uk or
e-mail: bookshop@enterprise.net for details.

To order please quote title, author and ISBN and your full name and
address. Cheques and postal orders should be made payable to "Bookpost
plc." Postage and packing is FREE within the UK
(overseas customers should add £1.00 per book).

Prices and availability are subject to change.